W9-ATC-625

xoxo to Mimi, Nana, Grandma Z, Betty, and Granny D.
– ED

To Maria and Melita; Vovó and Nana. May all the long-distance grandmothers in the world be able to visit and enjoy their grandchildren.
– LNP

As always, special thanks to KL & DW from ED & LNP

Kane Miller, A Division of EDC Publishing

For information contact:
Kane Miller, A Division of EDC Publishing
PO Box 470663
Tulsa, OK 74147-0663

www.kanemiller.com
www.edcpub.com
www.usbornebooksandmore.com

Library of Congress Control Number: 2016955633

Manufactured by Regent Publishing Services, Hong Kong, China
Printed June 2020 in ShenZhen, Guangdong, China

ISBN: 978-1-61067-617-5

4 5 6 7 8 9 10

Grandma's Favorite

Written by Erin Dealey
Illustrated by Luciana Navarro Powell

My grandma's favorite chair
has extra room for me.

The two of us play pirates
and we sail away to sea.

My grandma's favorite quilt
feels snuggly warm like hugs.

Inside, we make a secret fort.
Outside, we study bugs.

My grandma's favorite hat does not have fancy bows.
She wears it when she's fixing cars,

or in her workout clothes.

My grandma swings me off the ground.
We twirl and stomp our feet.

She shows me dances she loves best.

Our hands clap
to the beat.

The man with all
the flowers
runs Grandma's
favorite stall.

The orchid ballerina is
our favorite of them all.

In Grandma's favorite park,
there are no swings or slide.

Her favorite team is my team too.

Three CHEERS for Grandma's side!

My grandma's favorite song
would be too hard to pick.

Loud silly songs for work and play
and soft songs when I'm sick.

Oops! Grandma says my brown tree frog
is not her favorite pet.

She jumps each time he hops away.
(We haven't lost him yet!)

My grandma's favorite walk
is when she holds my hand.

She tells me ocean secrets.
Our toes dig in the sand.

My grandma's favorite treat
is big enough for two.

She gets an extra spoon for me.

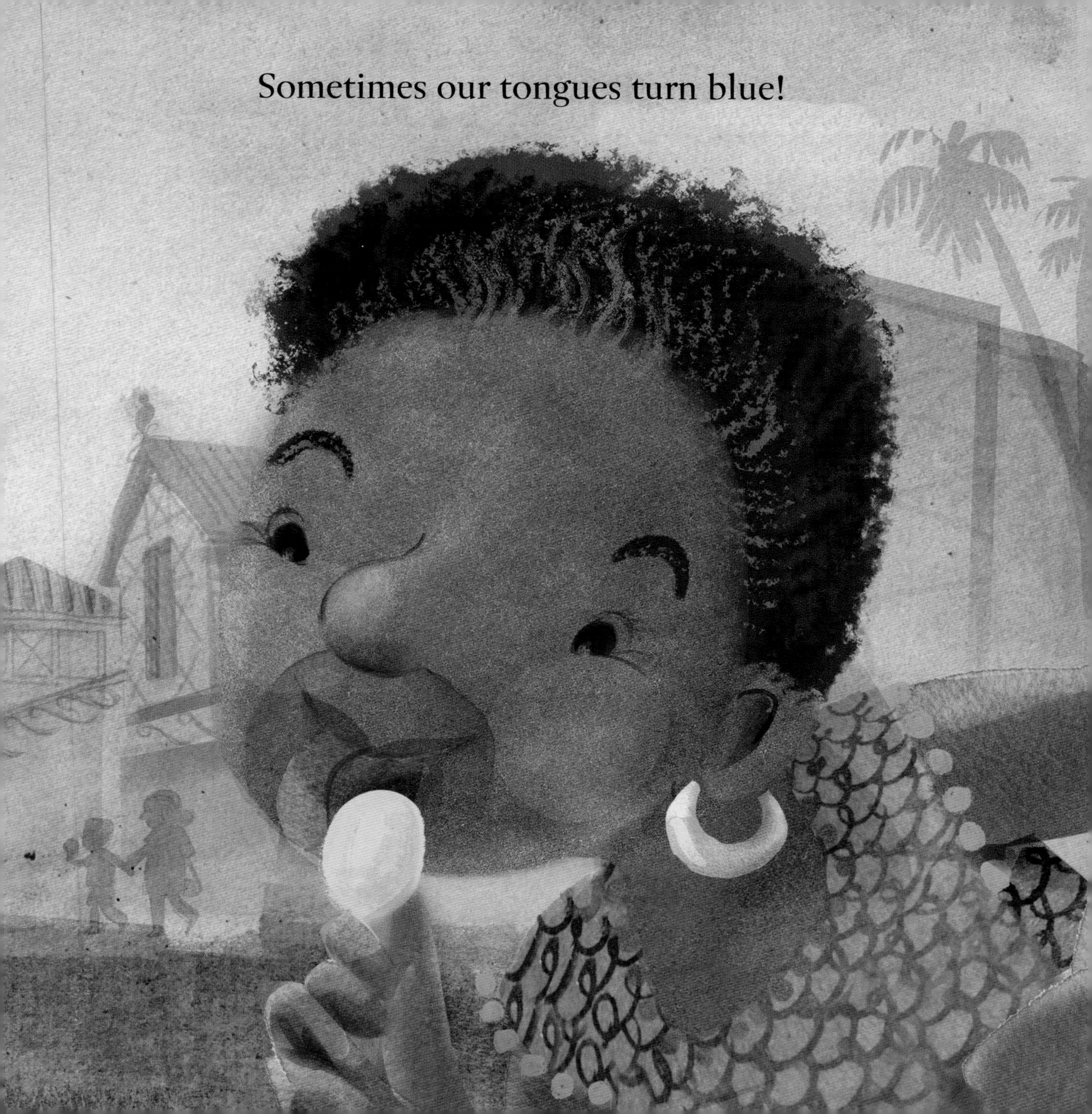

Sometimes our tongues turn blue!

After lunch my grandma says
it's time for us to rest.

I close my eyes and try,

but Grandma likes my naps the best.

My grandma's favorite bridge
is not for cars or trucks.

She plays the card game with her friends.
She says I bring her luck!

My grandma's favorite
words are:
"Love you to the moon!"

I send her fish-face kisses as she waves,
"I'll see you soon!"

My grandma's favorite book
keeps changing every night.

She loves to blow me one last kiss
when she turns out the light.

And even when she's far away,

she says the stars can see.

Her favorite time is anytime
my grandma spends with ME!